The Land of Selfs

by

M. H. Curtis

Published by: M. H. Curtis

ISBN: 978-1-7337992-6-3

Cover photo: Abhishek Bali

Dedicated to A Divine True Friend

Acknowledgements

There are so many people to thank for this work... Abhishek for the amazing cover photo, Gagan for editorial help and storyline input, Christine for editorial help, and of course the many people who have been inspirations for the various parts of the story. I would also like to thank the enlightened beings who help us on our way, help us to grow, help us to move forward! And last but not least, a big thanks goes out to you the reader, may you derive some benefit and enjoyment from the story...

M. H. Curtis

Contents

1) The Land

The Land of Selfs, often simply referred to as the "Land," was a happy land, a prosperous land, a land where everyone seemed happy and they all knew their place. Everyone, no matter what their position, nor how much accumulation each had, were welcomed as brothers and sisters of the same family. Because the Land was a growing country, the people could prosper if they worked hard. Their hard work would allow them to simplify their lives in some ways. Extra hard work gave them a little bit of extra pay, providing the ability to pay others to perform more menial tasks. This allowed the hard workers some time to devote to the arts or music or whatever their pastime pleasures.

Beyond a generation or two there wasn't much of a recorded history of the Land. In the Land, things had moved along at what seemed an "as usual" pace for as long as anyone could remember, and because there were no great changes in their past, remembering it didn't seem important.

Sure, the people of the Land knew their lineage. They also knew who the hard workers were because of the little things that the hard workers had that were not part of the life of all of the people. Those who did not have the little extra things bore no animosity towards those who did. This was because the people felt, if someone had something more they had earned it through their hard work.

The Land had a government and infrastructure, and to pay for it there were taxes. Everyone knew the taxes must be fair, because the government treated everyone equally and fairly and had the people's best interest at heart.

That was the way of the Land. Everyone felt good about what they had because there was abundance and all the people were able to have what they needed to live a complete and happy life, even if the lives of some of the people were a little more complete, and seemed a little happier than others.

The geography of the Land included: coastlines; and mountains; and valleys; and many places of natural beauty. Some of the valleys were backed by rugged mountains, and there were streams that meandered through valleys and picked up speed as they thundered over ledges creating lovely waterfalls. The coasts had both sandy beaches and rocky coastlines. The people in the Land felt that life could be no better, and it couldn't as far as they were concerned because that is what the media and government told them.

The economy of the Land was filled with businesses, educational institutions, and as already mentioned, a government with elected officials. There were also churches to help people find a higher meaning of life, and non-profit organizations created to help those people in need of help. Both the churches and non-profit organizations helped people without having a profit, nor a selfish motive.

Life in the Land was a great balance of society in a fine land. The businesses ranged in size from large production and service industries to single individuals performing services in small geographic areas. The educational institutions started with programs for very young children continuing through universities where degrees could be obtained to advance careers in business, or politics, or becoming an instructor at various levels within the school system itself, or any number of other career paths. The governments ranged in size from local governments where local matters were decided and local rules were established, to a large government of the land that was served through representation of an elected leader along with elected representatives of the regions. It also included a group of legal experts who were appointees and who interpreted the laws as the top tribunal of the Land.

In short, the Land of Selfs was not much different than the land where you and I live.

2) The Organizations

The Land contained a formal government system where representatives of the people were elected every few years. Along with the representatives of each region, a single leader for the entire Land was also elected. When elections were approaching, several people who wanted to become a representative, or the leader, undertook a campaign. During the campaign process the people seeking to be elected, proclaimed their qualifications and presented their view of how they could make the Land a better place, hoping to get enough votes of the people to represent their constituents.

In larger businesses a CEO (Chief Executive officer) was in charge of the business operations, and usually reported to a board of directors. The CEO climbed his/her way up through the organization with hard work, dedication, and collaboration. Many employees modeled themselves after the CEOs because they were dedicated to becoming a CEO themselves, a very prestigious event on the career path.

Religious organizations had leaders too. They are revered because of their spiritual insight and dedication to God. Often the parents of the religious leaders were also religious leaders, and so on and so on. It is believed that these families had inroads to God, and were the conduit through which God communicated with the common folk. Because of this belief the religious leaders had the unwritten support of the people, and as such the elected rulers respected them.

The educational institutions had their own hierarchy. Below the university level the leader was known as the superintendent. Below the superintendent were other administrators and managers at different levels and below them were the people responsible for the education of the children and young people. Because education was so important, the educational system was also highly regarded. Because of the general consensus about the importance of education, elected officials also respected the educational system and the decisions of the education leaders. The universities were set up more like businesses with each one having a president and a board to which the president reported.

Another group of organizations, ones set up to help people generally, were the not-for-profits. These were many independent organizations without a strong unity, because each organization competed for donations, which were limited.

However, because of the necessary roles these organizations played in the communities and in the Land generally, they were considered a good place to make donations. The nature of these organizations was also fashionable. In any year, certain types of not-for-profit organizations might be considered more fashionable to donate to than others. Because this perspective changed frequently, the donations continually moved throughout the variety of not-for-profit organizations as some came "into fashion" while others went "out-of-fashion." All in all, they were accepted as a necessary part of society to take care of niches that were not taken care of by any of the other organizations. The religious organizations were also not-for-profit, but they were busy keeping people on the path to a higher goal, and did not have the level of humanitarian work that other not-for-profits maintained.

3) Surprise Visit

One day something unusual happened. Strangers arrived on a ship from a faraway land. The ship was sighted out at sea, and because it had no weapons it was not viewed upon as an enemy. Because it was not viewed as an enemy, the proper thing to do was to welcome it to the Land with open arms. It was not often that visitors came and when they did, it provided the elected officials and other leaders the opportunity to unite as a group, each carrying the pride of the group they represented. This pride reflected the success of each group. Each was successful in their own way, and the success could be seen by the dedication of the workers. The workers also had the realization that if some workers were more successful and had a little more than others, it was because the more was earned. Having a little more was the motivation of many to work hard, so someday they might also have a little more, even if it meant working longer hours, or making tough decisions, or compromising in one area of their life so another might flourish.

The ship arrived at the port of the capital city and preparations were made for a large reception. Music, and dancers, and all sorts of other varieties of entertainment were brought together to welcome the honored guests, which no one had met, but all felt must be quite honorable, based on the size and condition of the ship. The ship was large by standards of the Land, and looked almost new, which was surprising considering it must have travelled a long way. It was impressive indeed and because it was, so were the preparations to welcome the new friends to the Land.

After a while, as the excitement grew, a narrow gangway was lowered by the ship and four people disembarked. They were few, and did not look like what might have been expected. They looked ordinary and their attire was not at all fashionable. It was assumed that these first people were representatives of a grand leader who sent the group as a preliminary introduction. Based on this assumption, the guests were greeted cordially but not with the respect or enthusiasm of a true leader.

The four individuals who came off the ship were met by dignitaries who escorted them to the secondary chambers of the rulers, often used to meet representatives of rulers or subordinates, but the primary chambers were used exclusively to meet and entertain the heads of the various groups, or on the rare occasion leaders of foreign lands who came to visit to discuss trade and other matters.

There were introductions among the four strangers and the representatives of the group leaders. After the introductions, the most unassuming of the four visitors addressed the representatives explaining that they had come from a distant land and one of them, himself, would like to learn from the various groups in the Land.

The representatives were delighted! When asked what his name was, he said simply that it was Sattva, and that they were from the Land of Chit. The leaders from the Land were amazed, not because of the extravagance of the name but rather because of the simplicity of it. Then Sattva was asked where their great leader was, assuming Sattva was only an ambassador of sorts.

Sattva smiled, "we have no one specific leader, where we come from, we are all equal. Some of us are teachers and some of us are students. Our goal in life is to learn, and so we request that I be allowed to stay and learn of your land and your society." The representatives of the groups smiled, all believing they could teach so much to this new visitor! The representatives went to their leaders and conveyed the discussion with the new visitors and the purpose of their visit. It was decided that the leaders would meet the guests the following day. In the meantime, they would discuss this request from their new friends and make plans for a welcoming dinner.

The guests were shown to accommodations. Sattva was the only one to stay and explained that the others would return to the ship. And so it was that Sattva became a special visitor to the Land.

4) The Internship

As arranged, the leaders met with Sattva the following day. After meeting with this new visitor, and making inquiries about what exactly he wanted, and the purpose of his visit, it was decreed that this would be a day of celebration.

During the initial meeting over brunch there were general discussions about the land and the major groups, and how all were successful. Presentations were made by the leaders from each group.

The leaders impressed upon Sattva how they were all revered by the people for their righteousness, for giving opportunities enabling people to rise to the top if they desired to do so through dedication and hard work, and because of the benevolence and transparent nature of the leaders themselves. Basically, they represented themselves reflecting that for all the leaders gave, the people loved them.

The representatives also found their guest interesting. He was gentle, quiet, kind, and had dark eyes that did not actually reveal much about him. Yet, all who met him felt good about him, comfortable with him, and were basically willing to answer any questions he asked without hesitation or consideration about whether the answers were proper, because they were honest. After the presentations, Sattva told the dignitaries that the presentations were impressive, and that he came to the land to learn about their organizations and the success of the groups. After making his request, Sattva sat down indicating that his request was concluded. The leaders suggested to

Sattva that they break and reconvene later in the day, before dinner. In the meantime they would discuss his request and they would be prepared to address his request when they reconvened.

Later that day all of the group leaders, their dignitaries, and Sattva met again. As Sattva waited patiently the elected leader told him the group leaders had unanimously decided to provide him, if he was willing, an executive internship in each of the groups. One selected organization from within each group would be chosen for the internship. Each internship would last from between 2 to 4 weeks depending on the size of the organization and the complexity of the organizational structure. At the end of the internships, they would have a live televised event for all the people to watch, what they were sure to be a monumental success and the beginning of a wonderful relationship with the Land of Chit. Sattva agreed to the executive internship plan and expressed his gratitude for their hospitality.

5) Business Internship

It was decided that the first internship for Sattva was in the business group. The leader of the business group was proud to be chosen first because he felt that among all of the groups, business was the most innovative and he wanted to leave a lasting impression in order to open the doors of opportunity to engage in trade with the Land of Chit. Sattva travelled to the location of the stellar business chosen for his internship. It was a manufacturing company that made state-of-the-art medical devices which aided in eye surgery.

Sattva's function as an executive intern was to observe the various departments within the organization and work with each one for a few days. He worked with the sales team first, discovering how the sales estimates were developed. He was surprised when he found out that most of the sales forecasts were based on estimates of the sales leader. As Sattva and the sales executive reviewed the forecast numbers the sales executive confided that estimates were based a lot on gut feel, and somewhat on historical interest in the product by potential customers, as well as potential sales that had been worked on for some time.

Then Sattva went to work with the engineering group for a few days. It was interesting for him because engineering was where the product development took place and as it turned out, the group was in the middle of developing a new product that would hopefully generate a continuing income stream for the company. The manager of the engineering group was glad to have Sattva join them. Sattva was a very likable person and comfortable to be around, and people opened up to him about what was going on. In engineering they had worked on developing many new products but kept missing the mark on the one that would fill the niche and provide the continuing income stream they were seeking.

In conversing about the development process Sattva discovered that the president of the organization had a habit of not being patient and often directed the engineering group to move on to new potential products before a current one had been perfected. Because of this process, the organization experienced huge cash drains without sustainable results to show for it. When Sattva inquired why this was the case, the engineering manager told him in confidence that the president received a percentage of the revenue from new product developments and continually searched for the successful one. Unfortunately, the president was an older man and had lost some patience due to his desire to find that one product that would boost his bonus and retirement income.

After finishing his time in engineering Sattva moved to the production department which included the materials and quality groups. The production workers were few and really knew their jobs well. The production manager was proud of the group and their dedication to high quality products produced on time. This meant that the group often put in a lot of overtime to meet shipment requirements for last-minute sales. On one of the days Sattva spent in the production department the department manager happened to be gone, and the president took it upon himself to give Sattva a tour of the production facility. The president was proud of the production effort, but admitted to Sattva that most of the production would eventually be contracted out to another company specializing in manufacturing. When Sattva inquired why, he was told in confidence that it would save a little money, and the savings would benefit the president's as well as some of the other company executives, bonuses and salaries. Having been led to believe that life in the Land was content and everyone was happy, this was something that tended to show a different side of life in the Land of Selfs.

Sattva took notes about the most basic things and asked a lot of questions. He was impressed with the manufacturing, and the dedication of many employees, but not impressed by some of the motivation behind the decisions being made.

At the end of his time with the manufacturing company, representing the best of the business group in the Land, Sattva was taken to dinner. The president and managers present all thanked Sattva for being an executive intern with their organization, and let him know he was welcome any time. The next day Sattva checked out of his hotel and travelled to his next internship with a non-profit organization.

6) Not-For-Profit Internship

Sattva took the weekend off between the two internships to explore some of the natural beauty of the land, and was ready to start his internship with the not-for-profit organization the first thing the following week. At the not-for-profit he met the executive of the organization, a woman who recently assumed the role. During their meeting the executive told him he would be attending meetings of the workers, who were caregivers for the elderly. He would also be reviewing the processes of fundraising as well as learning about the accounting for all of the different facets of the organization.

The meeting of the workers was the first thing on the agenda, occurring almost daily and where he would spend a bit of time over the next couple of weeks. At the first meeting he met many of the workers, and they were very nice. He also noticed that in discussing the different patients, the workers were quite serious and there was a tension or stress about them that was just under the surface of their personalities, and seemed to affect everything they did. This was interesting to him because he was not used to stress induced simply from living and dying, which were both part of life.

After the meeting, Sattva went to meet with the person in charge of the fundraising, which it turns out is a big part of non-profit work. Sattva learned the reason for fundraising being a big part of the not-for-profit organization was because donations were relied upon to "make ends meet." There was also the issue of there being limited donors with many not-for-profit organizations vying for the donations. So, the fundraising was in many ways like a game, trying to determine how to maximize donations, not only from outside donors, but also getting employees to donate more. After all, every little bit helped. The manager told Sattva about one example where the finance manager had donated to one employee, who was in competition with another employee to see who could raise the most money. The other person found out about the finance manager's donation and through a guilt tactic got the finance manager to donate to the other person and create a tie. Sattva thought it was interesting, using subterfuge, even among fellow employees to achieve a goal.

After his initial meeting with the manager of fundraising Sattva went to meet with the finance manager. It turned out that the finance manager was in the middle of budgeting for the new year and asked Sattva if he would be interested in helping with the budgeting process. Sattva was happy to help and began working on the file that budgeted benefits including health insurance and vacation accruals. For the next couple of weeks Sattva would go to meetings, learn more about the fundraising efforts, and work on the budget. It was toward the end of his internship that Sattva discovered several managers were accruing vacation pay at a rate that was higher than the organizational policy. Sattva asked the payroll processing person about it. Like everyone else, the payroll processing person felt very comfortable with Sattva and told him that the Human Resource manager, who also managed the payroll, initiated the increase when there had been a change in financial management.

Sattva met with the non-profit executive and discussed the findings of increased vacation pay for some of the managers, which even involved a payout in one case due to the retroactive application of the excess accruals. Upon inquiry, Sattva discovered the executive was told about the issue by the finance manager. Sattva inquired from the executive what would be done about the situation. The executive told him that she was relatively new in the position and would have a tough time pursuing the issue. She told him that taking action due to the improper vacation accruals would tend to drive a wedge in the organization rather than unite it around her, the new leader. Sattva asked for clarification because it was his understanding that if there was manipulation involved, instead of an error being the cause, such a manipulation was illegal and subject to penalties for the initiator. The executive concurred with Sattva but told him that making the information public, which may happen if there was legal action, would cast a dark cloud over the organization and adversely impact the fund-raising efforts. She went on to explain that it might cause an internal shake-up that would be too much for the organization to be subjected to. Instead, the solution would be to change back the accrual rates to what they should be, and the organization would go on. The executive even admitted that by taking this course of action and sweeping the issue "under the carpet," she would be complicit if it was ever discovered, but it was worth the risk since exposing it would also be a smudge on her career, and limit her ability to move on. She also confessed that by letting it go, the managers who had received the excess would be indebted to her, which is a nice place to be in a new position. Essentially, the managers "owed her one."

Sattva left the non-profit organization contemplating the risk of someone willing to break the law and cover something up rather than take a more correct, but perhaps tougher choice of allowing the law to work and fix the organization. He also wondered if a different tact would be possible using the exposure, and subsequent clean-up of the issue to show donors that a problem was found and responsibly taken care of. Sattva felt such an approach might end up making the organization an even stronger and a better place to donate.

7) Government Internship

The next internship for Sattva was with the main government. He was to be the executive intern for the elected leader of the Land. The leader decided this because he wanted to make a positive impression on Sattva in the hopes of gaining favorable trade agreements with the Land of Chit. He especially wanted to trade for certain minerals and other natural resources critical to the technological growth of the Land. Sattva was given an office and met with the leader midmorning on the first day of his internship. The leader welcomed him warmly and provided him a schedule of the things he would be engaged in for the next several weeks.

The schedule included spending time observing the elected representatives debate about the most important issues facing the people and how to best deal with them. The schedule also included visits to the government groups of trade, security, infrastructure, revenue, and other services. There was an appointment on the schedule showing that Sattva would be meeting with the leader two times a week, and the meeting was listed as a review session. During this, his first day however, he was having lunch with the leader after being given a general tour of the government which included being shown all of the areas where he would be spending time during his governmental internship.

During lunch with the leader that day, Sattva was very cordial while the leader discussed the trade opportunities.

Unlike his usual style, the leader even spoke of some of the trade they hoped to engage in, and highlighted the items high on the priority list. The leader realized he was showing all his cards in a game that normally was more akin to poker, yet he felt very comfortable with Sattva and he did not hold back any thoughts on any subject.

The next day was the beginning of internship Sattva was having with the Revenue department. The Revenue department was responsible for assessing and collecting taxes from the people and the businesses. They also were responsible for preparing the budget based on estimated revenues, and preparing many internal reports for other departments of the government. Sattva was also scheduled to spend time reviewing the taxes of the people and was slated to spend several days in the Revenue department. During his review, Sattva felt a good overview of the history of taxes would be in order. It took several days to pull all of the data together, but he finally created a summary of the history of taxes of the people on his last day at the Revenue department.

The summary showed, though spending by the central government remained relatively constant, the tax of the people went up gradually and the taxation of business entities generally went down about the same overall amount. Upon seeing this, he decided to inquire of the head of the revenue department if there were any changes in the spending by the government that might indicate an increase in the taxation of the people. When asked generally if the taxes remained relatively stable or if there were reasons that the taxes of the people might increase over time, the manager of the revenue department said he was not aware of any reasons why that might be the case. Because his last day with the revenue department was on a Friday, he made a note to himself to later inquire of the elected leader about the observation of the tax increase for the people and decrease for select business segments.

His next government internship was with the elected representatives in their large chamber where they held meetings and debates and votes about the issues of the people. One current issue related to assault weapons. There had not been any wars in the Land for as long as anyone could remember, and a majority of the general populace was of the opinion that common citizenry should not own assault type guns. Of course, there was a small but strong contingent of people in favor of assault weapon ownership, and the gun manufacturing businesses made great profits from sales of assault weapons, so needless to say there were some people who were not in favor of banning assault weapons.

After a few days of debate, the representatives of the majority seemed to win. A bill was passed that banned the sale of assault weapons, and the issue looked like it concluded in favor of the people. Sattva obtained a copy of the bill and read it that evening. The bill contained language that allowed assault weapon manufacturers to continue manufacturing the parts and pieces of assault weapons, which people could purchase and assemble the weapons themselves, which the law didn't prohibit. Though the bill had been touted a success for the people, after reading the text of the bill Sattva was of the opinion the bill was not the success indicated. In fact, the bill actually allowed the manufacturers of assault weapon parts to make a higher profit because the parts, on a piece-by-piece basis, generally sold for more than when assembled into a finished product. This also meant the manufacturers did not have to pay labor for the final assembly of the weapons. He also made a note to discuss this with the leader before leaving.

During the next several weeks Sattva had internships at other government departments. At each one he found that the way things seemed on the surface did not always represent the underlying results, as he had discovered in both the revenue branch as well as in the halls of the representatives of the people. On his last day he was scheduled for a lunch with the leader, who was happy to meet Sattva and review the internship of the government which the leader believed Sattva found to be exemplary.

Sattva expressed his concern about the increase in taxes of the people while correspondingly reducing taxes on some business segments, and then Sattva smiled and asked if the leader would help him understand. The leader also smiled and told Sattva that some businesses supported the government, and by that he meant the elected officials, more than others. He continued stating it seemed appropriate to reward the businesses for doing so, and that the increases to the people were very small, so all in all it was a good thing. The leader also took the same tact when Sattva brought up the bill regulating assault weapons, which seemed to do one thing, but actually did another. The bill intended to ban assault weapons actually ended up being even more profitable for the gun manufacturers.

Sattva left the government internship with a better understanding of the operations of government than he started with, though he was not really surprised. It seemed like the function of the government confirmed a belief he already had.

8) Educational Internship

The internship for Sattva in the educational group was to be in the office of the superintendent of a large school district. It was felt by the leaders that this would provide Sattva the best potential exposure to a broad section of the education system. Sattva started the following week and was the executive intern to the superintendent himself. At the school district Sattva was given a tour of the district office and also provided an agenda of the schedule of the superintendent. Then it was arranged for Sattva to visit several schools over the remainder of the week. During the following week there was a meeting, a public forum, to discuss the future needs of the district with the school board. The school board is a group of elected officials representing the public and directing the activities of the school district, much like a board of directors of a business.

For his first day, as had been the case with the other internships, Sattva had lunch with the executive he was working with. The superintendent had an approach to managing the requirements of the school system very similar to the business leader's approach in the medical device manufacturing company. The people were viewed as important resources, for the most part. It was an interesting revelation for Sattva, and yet he wasn't really surprised. The superintendent was a very nice man who seemed like he had a solid grasp of the requirements of the job. He had been in his position for several years and previously had worked as the principal of a school for a few years. This meant the superintendent was very familiar with the inner-workings of individual schools as well as the operations of the district office. He was a good fit for the position.

As the superintendent discussed the internship, he asked Sattva what he hoped to get out of the process. Sattva expressed that he, and the people of land from which he came, was interested in learning about the various groups that make up the society of the Land of Selfs, and the little details that made the various groups successful. Sattva, being a very likable person, also seemed to be very comfortable for the superintendent to associate with and be around. As the lunch progressed the Superintendent started discussing the board meeting that was taking place the following week. There was an issue very important to the school district to be presented. The superintendent told Sattva, almost 3 years earlier a special assessment had been voted on and passed by the people in the district to provide extra funds for some one-time educational expenses. Continuing, the superintendent explained that the money normally used for those expenses was "freed-up" and the spending of that freed-up money became very discretionary. The superintendent was going to make a case for continuing the special assessment for another 3 years. The superintendent confided in Sattva, it wasn't that the school district could not get by without it. The superintendent explained that once special assessments passed, by their very nature in support of schools, they were fairly easy to get voted for over and over.

At this point Sattva asked, "but because the purpose of these assessments are "special," doesn't it mean that they are generally presented as the need for them having limited duration and specific purpose?" The superintendent nodded in agreement. Then he explained that people tend to have short memories about this kind of thing and once the people get used to paying for something it was much easier to get them to keep paying. The superintendent continued to explain that all it meant was providing any number of justifications and it should be an almost guaranteed success, but the board would have to approve support for putting the measure back on the ballot.

The rest of the week Sattva spent time at several different schools, learning about curriculum. He also learned that with technological advances, the young people in the schools were spending less time outside and more time in front of a computer. At each school he asked if the curriculum included exercises designed for the students to make an inner search, to explore the silence of the inner person.

The answer was the same, that an inner, or spiritual search was not taught in the classroom.

The week flew by quickly and Sattva learned a great deal about the education system, both in how the schools operated and in the workings of the administrative function. The following week, on the day of the school board meeting, Sattva spent the day with the superintendent. During the day the superintendent again went over the sales pitch for extending the special assessment 3 more years. During this process Sattva was able to ask some clarifying questions.

The first question Sattva asked was if the school district needed the money on an on-going basis, why not just raise taxes? The answer was that the tax rates were decided by the people based on a property tax, a percentage of the value of the real property, voted on by the people that could not be changed without another vote of the people. Sattva thought about this answer for a moment and then asked, "isn't your district growing with a lot of new housing developments and if so, doesn't that generally increase property values, which would mean that the funding for the district is actually going up?" The superintendent's explanation was yes, currently the values and taxes were going up, and it was greatly benefitting the district, but it hadn't always been the case. He went on to explain that no one knew how long the increase would continue, but because the special assessment was such a windfall at the moment, it would be better to continue getting that benefit as well, even if the population supporting the school district were subject to increasing taxes due to increases in property values, in addition to the special assessment. The superintendent also explained that while most people knew taxes were up, most did not connect the dots to realize how much extra taxes were available to the school district. The superintendent confided that if the people did know, there would be no way the assessment would pass again, so selling the idea to the public had to be an appeal "for the kids." From his experience, this approach worked every time.

Sattva attended the meeting, and the pitch by the superintendent was accepted by the board. The board voted unanimously to move the assessment extension to the ballot in the next election. It turned out the next election was a primary election, so if the measure somehow lost, the district would have time to develop a different special assessment to include with the next general election. That would give them 2 chances to gain a special assessment and build up the reserve funds of the district like never before!

Sattva left the internship with the education group having a far better understanding of how things worked than he had when he started only a short time earlier. Sattva did not judge what was going on, but in reviewing and evaluating what he had learned, it seemed clear that the approach of the district was a bit more self-serving than he would have previously thought.

At this point Sattva had completed all of his internships and now it was back to the government capitol where he would spend some time organizing his notes from the internships and compiling the highlights into a presentation that would be given on a live telecast for the entire land to view.

9) The Preparation

All the land was abuzz about the strange visitor from the Land of Chit whom they had hosted for the past couple of months. There had been only positive information in the rumors spread, which meant that no negatives about the stranger were mentioned at all. It was the word everywhere that the interpretation could only mean, whatever the intention was of the "executive internship" sponsored by the Land, it was a huge success.

Sattva spent the week preparing his presentation to the leaders of all of the groups, the other people present. He was also aware that it would be broadcast to any people wanting to see it. He felt his task was simple, to express the important points of all he had learned in a straight forward and honest manner. He knew one or two major highlights of his internship at each group would be enough.

In the meantime, preparations for the televised event were under way in the capitol. One of the great halls was being readied for the presentation. There were cameras being set up, and enough seating to accommodate a large crowd. The elected leader, along with the group leaders were engaged in meetings. These meetings mostly centered around how successfully each of the internships had gone, and how impressed their new visitor must be with all of the obvious positive features of the Land. They also explored how the great courtesy they had all shown their visitor might be leveraged for beneficial trade terms, and how trade with the Land of Chit might help each one of their groups. At one point during the meetings the elected leader inquired if the ship from the Land of Chit had returned. It had left the port a couple of days after it arrived and had not been seen since. Word was that it was not back in the harbor, which provided even more enthusiasm for the group of leaders as it must surely mean that Sattva would stay to begin the trade discussions.

The citizenship all looked forward to the presentation. The leader of each group represented to Sattva that everything was done for the benefit of the people. The people themselves were accepting and comfortable with their leaders, and felt this would be the biggest and best representation of their land anyone of them had ever witnessed. The schools were the best they could be, the government with the elected officials working hard for the benefit of the people could not be any better, they reassured themselves. The businesses worked hard to keep the people employed and shared in the success of the business, because after all, without the workers the businesses could not succeed.

The non-profit organizations were the most beneficial that any could be, because they worked tirelessly at what they believed in, and because self-sacrifice was the nature of the people working for others. All in all, the Land was perfect and there could be no doubt that the same conclusion was being presented by the visitor.

During the time of his stay in the Land, Sattva found a local church to visit. He visited the church at some point every day he was in the area of the capital city.

He preferred evening time to visit the church, but with all of the festivities going on, he found himself tied up with engagements most of the nights during the week. Because of his schedule, he often would go to the church early in the morning when it was quiet and the land was in peace. Each day when Sattva went into the church the minister would greet him and Sattva would be courteous, exchanging pleasantries and then would sit alone and engage in what looked like prayer for extended periods of time. It was unusual for the minister to see a parishioner praying for long periods of time and so the minister developed curiosity about it over the several weeks Sattva went to the church for his prayer. On the day before the presentation, the minister engaged Sattva in a conversation, inquiring about his praying.

Sattva explained it was a type of prayer called meditation. Sattva asked the minister if the book of his God stated that God created everything and was everywhere. The minister replied that it did. Sattva told the minister the beliefs were the same in his land, and the people discovered through meditation God could be found within each person if they chose to seek God there. The minister was surprised as he had never had a parishioner discuss God in such a way. Sattva smiled as the minister reflected on what he had been told. Then the minister asked Sattva the meaning of his name and the name of the Land from where he came. Sattva told him that his name meant virtue, and the name of the Land, Chit, meant awareness. When the minister looked at Sattva again, instead of seeing just another person, the minister felt he was looking a someone who was very different, but he wasn't sure exactly why that was. Sattva smiling gave the minister a warm handshake and thanked him for being so courteous during his visits. As he turned to leave Sattva asked the minister if he planned on watching the presentation. The minister said that he normally would not but for this occasion he certainly would. Sattva left, going back to his hotel to provide the final preparations of his presentation.

10) The Presentation

The elected leader was the first to speak at the presentation. He spoke of the pleasure it was to have a new friend and representative from the Land of Chit, and all looked forward to having beneficial and rewarding trade with their new friends in the future. He extolled on the benefits their Land could offer, including all of the things Sattva came to learn about. He also mentioned what a wonderful executive intern Sattva had been for the government, how he was patient and a great listener, how he grasped concepts so quickly, and how his magnetic personality made him a trusted friend.

Next to discuss the executive internship was the group leader of business. He also gave Sattva great reviews, and was impressed how Sattva learned about the nature of business and profitability, and understood that the employees were the number one asset of a business. The business leader also was proud of the contribution they were able to share with Sattva about the keys to success of business, and looked forward to a long and prosperous trade agreement with the Land of Chit.

The not-for-profit leader was next, and talked about the great internship Sattva had with a leading not-for-profit organization. He spoke of the compassion Sattva showed in his dealings with the organization, and how it was impressed upon Sattva that everyone in not-for-profit organizations were self-sacrificing dedicated to helping others.

The education leader was next. He spoke of the awareness Sattva had about education and how he was able to both learn about their education systems, and impress the people in the schools themselves. He also talked about how important the people in the communities are and how the educational system is a balance between the needs of the students and the economy of the people generally. He expressed appreciation for the opportunity to have Sattva as an intern and hoped that the stellar nature of the education system would be embraced by

Sattva and the Land of Chit as much as it was in their Land.

Before Sattva was able to begin his presentation, the minister of the local church where Sattva had spent some time every day for the past many weeks, requested to speak. It was an unusual request but the elected leader, recognizing that no internship had been arranged for the religious group, was happy to oblige the minister, but of course only after reaching out to the religious group leader for his approval. The minister started out, "for the past several weeks, each day Sattva has come to spend time in the church. He has been as devoted in his belief as anyone I have ever met, and I am convinced he is a true man of God. He is a man of virtue from the land of awareness. The opportunity to observe this guest and briefly converse with him has been a blessing." Being a man of few words, the minister's comments were complete and Sattva approached to speak, smiling at the minister as he left the podium.

Sattva began, "it was intended that I provide a formal presentation to accompany my talk, but I have not done so and ask your forgiveness and understanding." He paused for a moment and continued, "it will be clear why I did not make that preparation in a few minutes. Now I will discuss each internship including what I learned, and what was revealed through my experience."

As he paused again, the crowd, including the leaders, were all poised waiting with excitement, expecting that they were about to hear how great they all are, and how much Sattva gained from his experience.

Sattva said, "In the internship for the business group I learned that the jobs are sometimes outsourced so the leaders can have the 'more' that everyone takes for granted they earn, but it actually comes through sacrificing employees by the business leaders." Sattva went on, “I also learned that money is spent irresponsibly as directed by the organization leader for the development of new products providing an income stream, but development is rarely allowed to be completed due to impatience, and the desire to have an increased income stream as soon as possible because the compensation of the executives are based in part on increased revenue."

The entire room and gallery were quiet after hearing those comments, and the silence gave Sattva the opportunity to speak again.

"In the not-for-profit group, sometimes people find it easy to get their 'more' by giving themselves more than they are entitled to, and the leaders look the other way because they do not want the stain of impropriety upon their hands. Those people who take advantage of their positions rather than being selfless are actually selfish. If a selfish act should occur, I discovered that it may become leverage for all to join in the activity of malfeasance by being complicit, rather than following the law. This is a course chosen by them rather than nipping the problem in the bud and providing the leadership the opportunity to be the worthy leaders of the organizations they represent themselves to be. This is what I learned at the non-profit where I was an executive intern."

Again, there was a quiet in the room allowing Sattva to continue, "in the education system, to work around the limits of taxes, special assessments are requested for special funding, but the school leaders know that once an assessment is in place, it is easily kept there and the school districts push for them to continue, even if their share of tax revenue is increasing faster than the expenses due to rising property values and growth. Rather than a balance, they actually create additional burden for the taxpayers using the guilt of the needs of the children as the leverage for their greed. One additional point about the education system is that it does not promote the students with a foundation for an inner search or exploration. This inner search we find to be the actual foundation of truth in the Land of Chit."

Sattva then continued because everyone was so surprised, no one had said a word. "Lastly, what was learned about the government was, laws touted to benefit the majority of the people actually benefit the minority, as was the case in the recent law making the sale of assault weapons illegal. The same law is allowing for the sale of the parts of assault weapons so people can assemble the weapons themselves, which also is providing the manufacturers to make more profits. Another thing I learned is that the continual rise in taxation of the people is balanced with a reduction in the taxes for businesses so that officials will benefit from business relationships when they leave office." As Sattva was saying this last bit about the government, the elected leader jumped up in protest, and demanded the cameras be shut off and that Sattva be apprehended for making false claims against the Land. At that point all of the leaders were chiming in with the elected leader for a stop to the atrocity Sattva was presenting.

Then something quite unexpected happened. As everyone watched and the cameras continued to record, and much to the surprise of the leaders who thought to punish Sattva for his remarks even though he was a visitor, Sattva's body developed a glow and it gradually disappeared before their very eyes. At this point, everyone became very anxious. Sattva however, although invisible to the people of the Land, continued to speak. "I along with my brethren in the Land of Chit all are decedents of people who left this Land a few hundred years ago to pursue true freedom, a spiritual life without greed. What I came here to learn was if life here in the Land had changed. I discovered essentially that it has not. The people continue to work hard for "more," but the leaders manipulate and control them for their own selfish benefit. Until you understand the transcendental nature of life, that we are not individuals separate from one another but are all connected, instead of a land of unity you will indeed remain the Land of Selfs. For any who hear this message and understand, when your desire to find your spiritual self is strong enough, and you have the will to abandon the material world, a way will be found for you to join us in the Land of Chit."

At that point, Sattva was gone and all the people throughout the land were astonished by his revelation about how the leaders were conducting their groups as well as treating the people.

Of course, immediately after the presentation many news and press releases were presented stating that Sattva was a saboteur, intending to break up the Land in preparation for an invasion to conquer the people and take over the resources and technology. After enough of the propaganda was spread, eventually people started believing it. Yet a few people, people who were not leaders, people who had met Sattva and understood that he was telling the truth, began to explore what he meant by a spiritual self.

Over the years, quite a number of people disappeared including the minister who had met and talked with Sattva, but because those people were of little consequence to the materially oriented leaders of the Land, their disappearance was not news worthy and the rest of the people in the Land of Selfs continue in their way of working hard to get more...

www.ingramcontent.com/pod-product-compliance
Lightning Source LLC
LaVergne TN
LVHW091011080826
845145LV00003B/1225

* 9 7 8 1 7 3 3 7 9 9 2 6 3 *